The Goblin of Tara

OISÍN MCGANN

For the Rogans of Kells,
County Meath – the Royal County

First published in 2007 in Great Britain by
Barrington Stoke Ltd
18 Walker Street, Edinburgh, EH3 7LP

www.barringtonstoke.co.uk

This edition first published 2013

ISBN: 978-1-78112-222-8

Printed in China by Leo

Contents

Chapter 1
The Night of Halloween

Long ago, people thought that on Halloween, the gates of the Otherworld opened for that one night of the year. Then the souls of the dead sometimes came across into our world, where they roamed as ghosts and tried to contact the living.

And sometimes, on Halloween, other things crossed over to our world too.

This is the story of the Goblin of Tara and the terror he spread across the land.

Thousands of years ago, Ireland was ruled by many kings and queens. Each king or queen had their own land where their people hunted, grew crops and kept cattle. Every ruler was a great warrior. They had to be because they were always fighting with the other kings and queens about little corners of land. Sometimes they fought because one king had stolen another king's cows. And if you fight a lot, you have to get very good at it or else you die.

There were no armies back then. If someone invaded your land, you all had to get stuck in and help fight them off.

When these kings and queens weren't fighting, they liked to have big feasts. Then they could boast about the great battles they'd fought. They often lied to make themselves seem stronger and braver than in real life, but as long as there was plenty of good food and drink and a place to sit close to the fire no one minded. Anyway everyone liked a good story, even if it wasn't all true.

Cormac MacArt was the greatest king of the time – the High King. He was a fine warrior and an even better storyteller and his bards, his musicians, played the best music. He lived in a ring-fort on the Hill of Tara, and everyone from miles around could see it. Every Halloween, he had a massive feast where he told his stories (which were mostly true). People sang and danced and played hurling and had fights. They had a really good time. 'Having a bit of crac', they called it.

On this year, there was a new face in the High King's fort. Finn MacCool was a tall, strong young man with blond hair and a serious look in his eyes. He was here because the Fianna were at the feast and he wanted to join them. The Fianna were the greatest warriors in Ireland. Their chief was the mighty Goll

MacMorna. Finn had tried to join them many times already, but Goll never let him.

Goll and his brothers had killed Finn's father many years before and the Fianna leader did not trust this fierce young man. Finn was still only a teenager, but he'd already won great respect for his fighting skills.

Goll suspected Finn wanted revenge for his father's death. And he was not wrong. Finn had a terrible hate for Goll, but he wanted to join the Fianna more than anything in the world. Revenge could wait. And so Finn MacCool came to the Hill of Tara to try and join the Fianna.

Poets and story-tellers, musicians and dancers, hunters and farmers, druids and warriors, everyone came to Tara for Cormac's feasts. They even came on Halloween. They came even if they knew the goblin would come too, across from the Otherworld.

Every year, the goblin came to set fire to the ring-fort on Tara. No one had ever defeated it. No one had even seen it close up. When the goblin came near, it played a terrible lullaby, which put everyone to sleep. And while they slept, the goblin burned their homes. It had done this every year for seven years.

But still people came to Tara for Halloween. Life was hard in those days. Sometimes it was worth risking your life for a bit of crac.

Chapter 2
The Witching Hour

As evening turned to night, more people came to King Cormac's feast and torches were lit to fill the fort with the glow of firelight. His people brought the animals inside the walls of the fort for the night to protect them from wolves.

In the great hall, there were piles of rich food to eat and barrels of mead to drink, but no one was hungry. Some people just drank until they passed out. Others talked too much or giggled like children even when the jokes weren't that funny.

Most of the warriors drank nothing at all as the night went on. They listened for any sound of warning from the guards watching outside. They kept their weapons beside them, for it was close to midnight.

The witching hour was near.

Finn's plate was filled with potatoes and the meat of deer and wild boar, but he was too nervous to eat much. He stared at the people sitting at the tables around him. He could see fear on their faces. He leaned over to talk to Goll, who sat at the top table. The Fianna's leader was an enormous man with long grey hair and a bushy beard, and an ugly scar across his left eye which was shut and blind.

"Do you think he'll come this year?" Finn asked.

"He comes every year doesn't he?" Goll grunted. "And every year it's worse."

Cormac MacArt stood up and banged his knife on the table so everyone stopped to listen. The High King was tall and burly, with red hair and beard and a face scarred from battle. The crowd became silent until the only sound was the massive fire crackling in the middle of the hall.

"Midnight is almost upon us," Cormac boomed. "I want every man to get his weapons and go up onto the walls of this fort. The goblin will not get inside this time. I will give my best bull to the man who brings me the monster's head. Death to the goblin!"

"Death to the goblin!" the men shouted.

They roared a mighty battle-cry and jumped to their feet. They grabbed their swords, shields and spears, they hugged their women and said goodbye to their children.

Their dogs barked with excitement, keen for action. The warriors stormed out of the great hall and past the huts outside it, onto the wall all round the fort.

The wall was made of earth and stones, and it had a fence of sharp wooden posts around the top. It was as tall as two men and around the outside was a deep ditch. It was built to defend against human attackers and it was built well.

But MacMeena the Goblin was no human.

Chapter 3
A Horrible Lullaby

Beyond the first ditch outside the fort wall, there was a second one. On the far side of this there were torches burning on wooden posts so that the men could see anything that came up towards the fort. But outside the circle of light, the darkness looked even more terrifying. As Finn got up onto the wall and stood ready to fight, he looked to his right and left and saw the men of the Fianna on both sides of him. He was proud he had this chance to fight with them.

These were the greatest warriors in Ireland. They had fought in hundreds of battles and defeated all sorts of enemies. But the goblin was different. In the seven years that the monster had haunted the Hill of Tara, they had never killed him. No one had even got a proper look at him.

Was everyone else as nervous as Finn was? He didn't know. He started to sing softly. Fiacha, an old friend of his father's, stood next to him. Fiacha was small and thin. His brown hair and moustache were turning grey. He'd fought with the Fianna for most of his life and was still as hard as stone. He saw Finn looking at him.

"What are you going to have for breakfast?" Fiacha asked him.

"What?" Finn said with a frown.

"Breakfast," said Fiacha. "What are you going to have?"

It was a silly question, but Finn saw it was better to think about his breakfast than the goblin.

"Porridge with honey," he said. "And some fried bread."

Finn was fond of honey.

"I'm going to have a wild boar steak with some eggs," Fiacha told him.

"I'm happy for you," Finn answered.

Suddenly the dogs started to howl. The cattle, goats and pigs began making noise too. Finn heard music – it was a creepy tune, like a lullaby you might play for a dead child. The music was being played on a harp.

"He's coming!" someone shouted. "MacMeena is coming!"

Finn lifted the shield on his left arm high and gripped his spear with his right hand. He was trembling as he stared out into the darkness to try and spot the monster. The harp music grew louder.

Finn's breathing grew faster and faster but he tried to stay calm. Then he saw that he wasn't trembling at all. It was his spear. It was vibrating as if someone had just hit it hard. Then the spear stopped and was still. Now Finn felt a shudder in the metal of his shield – and in the sword that hung from his belt. The goblin was coming closer.

His sword and shield stopped vibrating and then it seemed as if Finn's bones were trembling instead. As the music grew louder, his ears started to hurt. The pain spread into his skull and he closed his eyes and gritted his teeth. Tears welled in his eyes.

"What kind of magic is this?" he gasped.

"He's here!" Goll shouted. "Stand strong, men! Stand strong!"

With a huge effort, Finn opened his eyes. Beyond the wall, just on the edge of the light from the torches, stood a dark hunched shape. It was playing some sort of harp. Each note of the sweet, sad music beat into Finn's head as if his skull were a drum. All around him, he heard yells of agony. The pain in his own skull was terrible. It began to spread down his back and into his legs. He could only keep standing if he held hard onto his spear. All around him, men began to fall.

"Stand strong!" Goll roared again.

But it was no good. One by one, the warriors crumpled to the ground. Finn let out a tormented scream. He bent over like an old man, his fingers slipped down his spear. He could just make out the hunched thing as it began to walk up towards the fort. He screamed again. The music from the harp strings thudded

like hammer-blows inside his head. Then everything went black.

Chapter 4

Smoke and Meat and Death

When Finn woke he could smell burning flesh. He struggled to come back to his senses. When he opened his eyes he saw flames creeping across the back of the man who lay next to him. It was Fiacha. The older man woke up and started thrashing and yelling. Finn pulled off his own cloak to beat out the flames … and then he saw his own feet were on fire too.

"Aagh!" he yelped as he tried to put out the flames.

He pulled out his dagger and cut his boots off just as the fire began to move up his legs. It was only then that he looked up and saw what was happening around him.

His boots had caught fire because they were touching the fence that stood on the top of the earth wall. All the way round the wall, fire was burning up the fence. In some places, the flames were spreading to the bodies of the warriors who lay half-dead on the ground beside it.

Once he'd put out the flames on Fiacha's body, Finn started to take off his friend's boots.

"Mother Earth!" Fiacha yelled. "It's bad enough I'm burned to a crisp without you stealing my boots!"

"Stop your bleating, you'll have them back in no time," Finn told him.

He pulled the boots off Fiacha's feet and strapped them on. Then he rushed to help fight the fire. Fiacha wouldn't need his boots – he was too badly hurt even to stand up.

The burning fort lit up the night. Women screamed as they struggled to save their children. The goblin had set fire to all the buildings as the people lay helpless. Finn could see burned bodies in some of the huts. The black, burned shapes of dead dogs lay in the doorway of what had once been the great hall.

There was nothing left of the hall's straw roof. The rafters and the carved wooden posts were all that remained of the great hall. They jutted out of the smoking ashes like a burnt skeleton. Half the farm animals lay dead in their pens.

People were beginning to wake. They raced to fight the fires, but it was too late. The fort was finished. Finn worked with the others. Together they dragged people out of the flames and threw water on anything that was still on fire. They tried to help those that were hurt.

Everything smelled of smoke and meat and death. As the flames died down, the darkness crept over the fort and torches were lit once more. Finn slumped onto the ground. He just sat there, worn out. His face, arms and legs were scorched and black with soot.

The goblin had attacked many times before, but never like this. This time the monster had nearly destroyed them all. As he looked out at the bodies laid out on the ground in front of him, Finn hung his head and wept until he had no more tears to cry.

He had sworn to protect these people and he had failed.

"What is this curse?" he hissed. "Why does the monster do this?"

"Who knows?" a voice said from behind him.

It was Cormac. The king looked as weary as Finn and just as unhappy.

"It's a demon from the Otherworld and it wants the Hill of Tara as its own," Cormac went on. "Who knows why? But it will keep coming until there is nothing left of us. And I will not give in to it. Tara has been the High King's fort for as long as anyone can remember. I will not be the king who loses it.

We will re-build the fort and when the goblin comes next year, we will be ready for it. I swear to Mother Earth that I will have that thing's head on a post before the next Halloween is over."

Finn said nothing. Staring at what was left of the king's home, he began to think that Cormac MacArt might be mad.

Chapter 5
The Goat-skin Drum

Finn stayed at Tara with the Fianna to help Cormac's people re-build his fort. Then the Fianna left to hunt and roam around the forests of Ireland as they always did.

As winter fell, Finn spent more and more time in the Slieve Bloom mountains where he had grown up. He lived by hunting and slept in woods and caves. The goblin's attack haunted all his thoughts. Whenever he stared into his camp fire, he saw the people who had burned. His sleep was shattered by terrifying nightmares.

When the snows came, Finn left the woods and travelled south to Kerry to visit his family there. They soon saw how he'd changed. He spoke very little and smiled even less. He never stopped training with his sword and spear but he no longer seemed to care about any of it. Finn had always talked about his dream of joining the Fianna and how he hated Goll MacMorna, the Fianna chief. But now he never talked about it.

The only time he seemed to come alive was when the bards played their songs. The music lit up his eyes, but still he didn't smile. Winter turned to spring and spring turned to summer. The fine weather meant long, wonderful hunts across the wild Kerry hills. But Finn did not join them.

People started to say that the goblin's attack had destroyed him – that he was no longer a true warrior. But no one said it to his face, of course. Finn's sword arm was as strong as ever.

Instead of going hunting, he stayed in the village and learnt music from the bards. And still he did not smile.

He didn't smile until the day he saw a hairy little old man playing a drum Finn had never seen before.

It was made from a goat-skin which was pulled over a round wooden frame. The old man held it on its edge and beat the front of the drum with a little wooden peg that he had in his right hand. He pressed his left hand against the back of the skin. When he moved his left hand around the skin, the sound of the drum changed. Finn sat out near the wall and listened to this man play. When the music was finished, Finn's face split into a big grin.

"What's this drum you're playing?" he asked.

"It's called a bodhrán," the old man said, and he said the drum's name like this –

'bow-rawn'.

"Will you teach me?" asked Finn.

"I will," said the man and smiled back at him.

Chapter 6
A Deal with the King

Finn stayed in Kerry until the autumn and then he said goodbye to his family and headed out north, towards Meath and the Hill of Tara. The journey took many days across hills and wild woods, but Finn liked walking by himself. It gave him peace.

When he got to the High King's fort, he found the Fianna were already there. They were working with the king's men to try and make the fort even stronger. The wall was taller this time, the fence was thicker and the ditches were deeper. Finn was welcomed into the fort. There were fewer warriors this year – people said the goblin could not be beaten.

It was three days before Halloween.

Finn's friend, Fiacha, was still hurt from where he'd been burnt last year. He was sitting on a stool outside the great hall and wrapped in a cloak as he watched the rest of the Fianna work. He smiled when he saw Finn coming towards him, but it was a sad smile. Finn could see burn scars on his friend's neck and up the side of his face. His left hand was so twisted and scarred, it looked more like a bird's claw.

"You shouldn't have come," Fiacha said to Finn. "We won't win this fight. And I think that anyone who tries will only die for their trouble."

"You can be sure I didn't come here to die," Finn told him.

"Then you should go home," Fiacha said, looking up at him. "But I know you won't. You're too much like your father. He was a stubborn eejit as well. Here, I have something for you."

He grunted in pain as he reached behind him. He picked up his spear and handed it to Finn.

"This was your father's. He gave it to me as he lay dying – after Goll and his brothers struck him down. I'll stand on the wall with the rest of the lads on Halloween, but I'm in no state to fight. You should have this weapon now. It's yours by right. It's said to have magic powers, and anyway, it will bring you luck."

Finn nodded his thanks. 'How can this be such a lucky spear?' he thought. After all, it hadn't saved his father. He gave Fiacha his own spear in return and then strode towards the great hall. He left his bag, spear and shield outside and stepped into the warm dark hall. Cormac, the High King, and Goll MacMorna were sitting at a table, making plans to fight the goblin.

"What are you doing in here, boy?" Goll asked. "Get out!"

"I'm here to speak with my king," Finn snapped back. "And since I'm not a member of the Fianna, I don't have to answer to you, Goll MacMorna."

Goll stood up from the table.

"Mind your manners when you speak to me!" he growled.

"Eat my boots, you old fart!" Finn sneered.

Goll was fast. In the blink of an eye, he drew his sword and swung it up to Finn's throat. But Finn was faster. His sword hit Goll's with a clash of metal as it came up and swept it away. Then Finn stepped back and put his sword up again – ready to fight.

"Enough!" Cormac roared. "You're acting like fools! What do you want, lad?"

"I'm here to kill the goblin," Finn said as he put his sword down. "And if I succeed, I want what's coming to me."

"Any man who kills the goblin will have my best bull, as I said," Cormac grunted.

"I don't want your bull," Finn told him.

"Let me guess," Goll snorted. "You want to be allowed to join the Fianna."

"No," Finn replied softly. "I want to be leader of the Fianna. And when I am, you can swear that you'll be loyal to me or you can quit Ireland forever, you bloody dog."

"The boy's lost his mind!" Goll shouted.

"If you kill the goblin, you'll have what you want," Cormac told him. "I promise you that." Then Cormac turned to Goll. "And you'll agree too, MacMorna, for he'll be a better man than you if he succeeds ... Not that I expect him to."

Cormac leaned back against the table and looked down sadly. It was the first time

Finn had ever seen the High King show any weakness.

"This thing has haunted my kingdom for nine years," Cormac said. "And with every year that passes, his attacks grow worse. When MacMeena comes this Halloween, I think it will be a miracle if any of us live to see the morning."

Chapter 7
From Out of the Darkness

The warriors did what they could to be ready for the goblin's attack. On the morning of Halloween, they began to pour water over the fort and its fence to make them difficult to burn. Even the ground around them was soaked in water. As night fell, they did the same with their thick tartan cloaks – they soaked them in water to protect against the goblin's fire. Then the men stuffed their ears with wax to help them resist the goblin's music.

That night the animals were not herded into the fort. Instead, the younger boys led them far from the hill. Inside the ring-fort, the Halloween feast was held as normal. But no one was able to eat or drink with any enjoyment. The people sang sad songs and tried not to think about how scared they were. No one wanted to say that they should go away and leave the Hill of Tara to the goblin, even if many thought it to themselves.

But there wasn't a man or woman in the fort who would leave their king.

It was close to midnight. Finn joined the rest of the men on the wall. He saw the women and some of the older children come up the steps to stand with the men. He could understand why. The wall was as safe as anywhere else.

No one spoke. Finn could hear people near him trembling and breathing loud and fast because they were so scared. He knew how they felt. He had come here with a plan, but he couldn't be sure if it would work, or if it would kill him even faster.

Finn lifted his spear high and then jammed it down into the ground at his feet. He drove it in so hard that it stood up on its own. It was so deep into the ground that the spear-head was just above his face. He gripped the spear in front of him and waited.

"That's no way to treat a good spear," the man beside him said.

"If you're wise, you'll do as I do," Finn told him.

"I find I fight better when I don't have to dig my weapons out of the ground," the man said with a snort.

Finn didn't answer him. It was true – he did look stupid. He fell silent and waited. They all waited and stared out into the still darkness.

The only noises that they could hear along the wall were the odd cough, feet shifting about and the sound of someone singing very softly to a child.

Then the music began.

"MacMeena!" someone shouted in alarm. "The goblin is coming!"

"Mother Earth, give me strength," Finn whispered.

He pressed the flat of the spear-head to his brow and closed his eyes. The music grew louder. He could hear the vibrating in the air, in the fence and the wall, in the metal of his weapons. The vibrating felt its way into his flesh to his bones. Still Finn kept the spear pressed on his head. The cool metal gave him comfort.

Last year, every note from the goblin's harp had beat on his skull as if his head were a drum. And so Finn had spent the year learning about music. He learned how sound travelled, and how some musical notes could affect how people felt.

Finn thought about the old man he'd met, who played that strange drum. He remembered how the old man pressed his hand against the drum-skin to dull the sound of the drum. That was why Finn was pressing the spear against his forehead now. He hoped it would stop the harp music vibrating in his head.

Chapter 8
The Goblin's Tongue

The music swept over the people, a horrible sad lullaby that sent shivers down their spines. Finn felt the pain start in his head but as he looked quickly at the other warriors, he saw they were already crumpling. One by one, they clutched their heads and fell to the ground with loud cries of pain. Finn's head throbbed with the sound of the harp, but he still felt strong. He looked past his spear into the darkness beyond the fort. Just past the line of torches at the second ditch, he saw the goblin.

It was coming towards the gate.

"MacMeena is here!" Finn yelled.

But there was no one to hear him. All around him, the finest warriors in Ireland, and the people they were guarding, lay limp ... helpless. Finn stood alone and his head was pounding with the awful music of the harp.

MacMeena the goblin could see him now, standing alone on the wall. The goblin jumped over the ditch in one bound. He walked up the road and stood in front of the gates to the fort. He was still playing his harp.

This was no normal harp. It was made of his own hair and there was no frame for it. The goblin had a long head, almost like a horse. His beard had been stretched from his chin and neck and knotted with the hairs on his chest to make the harp.

As Finn stared at him, the goblin opened his mouth and out came a long, long tongue. Flames dripped from it like spit, and it licked the wooden gates of the fort. Where his tongue touched the wood, fire burst across it.

In a few heart-beats, the gates fell with a crash of smoke and sparks. As they broke up, the goblin stopped playing his music and walked through the flames into the fort.

He had blue skin and a head of wild black hair. His legs were like a dog's and his body was thin but strong. Now the music had stopped, Finn felt safe to take his head off the spear. A great anger started to build up inside him. The goblin turned and glared up at him.

"What kind of a man are you?" the goblin asked. "How can you stand the sound of my music?"

"I am Finn MacCool," Finn answered with a snarl. "And I cut the heads off bad musicians!"

He pulled his spear out of the ground and jumped off the wall to land in front of the goblin. MacMeena lashed out his tongue and hit Finn's shield. The shield was cut in two by the heat and Finn dropped it just in time.

Even as he did, he drove his spear into the goblin's chest. The creature screamed and fell back, pulling the spear out of Finn's hands. Finn drew his sword and held it up. He didn't want that fiery tongue to burn him.

The goblin ripped the spear out of his chest and tossed it away. His tongue struck out again like a whip and Finn whirled his wet cloak in front of him. It took most of the heat, exploded into flames and burned Finn's leg. Finn threw it to one side. Now he had nothing to protect himself from the goblin's fire.

"I've killed hundreds of heroes like you, boy," MacMeena hissed. "And I'll kill hundreds more!"

The goblin dragged his claws across the strings of his harp and Finn screeched in pain as he felt his bones shake inside him. He fell to his knees, but he swung his sword just as the goblin's tongue lashed out at him. It sliced into the tongue, but the sword was cut in half as well. MacMeena screamed and fell back, his mouth spitting sparks.

Finn dived forward and slashed at the goblin with what was left of his sword. He cut the strings on the goblin's harp and there was a noise like a hundred cats wailing.

The goblin screamed again and pounced on top of Finn as he tried to get up. Finn pushed the monster's mouth to one side just before the flaming tongue could sweep across his face. He grabbed the last bits of MacMeena's beard and wrapped them around the goblin's snout so that he'd tied MacMeena's mouth shut.

Finn kicked the monster away. The goblin fell back. He clawed at his mouth as he tried to get his tongue free. Without his magic weapons – the harp and the fiery tongue – the goblin couldn't fight. Finn jumped up and charged again. His leg was hurt and he only had half a sword, but his anger turned him into a monster too. His eyes bulged, his teeth seemed to grow like fangs and his muscles squirmed under his skin like big snakes. The goblin stared at him in terror and then turned and ran.

The evil goblin was fast – much faster than Finn with his burnt leg. Finn did not chase after him. Instead, he walked over to his father's spear and picked it up. The goblin was vanishing into the distance, almost hidden by the darkness. Finn could smell its blood and it drove him even wilder. But he didn't chase the goblin.

There was a fairy fort on a hill nearby. It was a gate-way into the Otherworld and Finn knew that MacMeena would use it to escape. He waited with his spear ready. At last, the goblin untied his beard and opened his mouth. Finn could see the flicker of flame from his tongue and then he aimed his spear. He hurled it as hard as he could. Out in the darkness, he heard a screech.

He walked out over the grass, towards the sound of growling. He found the goblin pinned through his leg by the spear. It was stuck in a tree and the monster was struggling to pull it out. He didn't see Finn until it was too late. His tongue twisted like a burning whip, but Finn's sword was faster and with a thud it hit the tree. MacMeena's blood spattered across the grass as his head fell from his neck.

Chapter 9
Goll MacMorna's Choice

One by one, the people of Tara woke up.
Many of them thought they'd never wake again.
Goll MacMorna sat up and blinked. He was lying
on top of the wall near the gate. Looking up
at the gateway, he saw a large ugly blue head
hanging from its wooden arch. The gates had
been burned, but the fort and its walls were
still standing.

Sitting on the wall by the gate was Finn
MacCool. He looked tired, and a broken sword

hung from his hand. But he was staring at Goll with a sly smile on his face.

"The goblin is dead, Goll," he called. "Your time is over."

Goll stood up, picking up his sword. Finn stood up to face him, his own weapon at the ready. All around them, the people were getting to their feet and coming to see what would happen next. The crowd was whispering and watching. Finn MacCool had killed the goblin. Now Goll had to swear loyalty to him or leave Ireland forever. But Goll was stubborn. No one knew what he'd do next. Cormac MacArt pushed through the crowd, but he didn't try and get between the two warriors.

Goll gripped his sword. Then he stood it on its point and knelt in front of Finn. He bowed his head.

"My sword is yours to command, Finn MacCool, Leader of the Fianna!" he said.

"And I will need it, Goll MacMorna," Finn answered.

The crowd gave a huge cheer. They rushed forward and Finn was pulled from the wall and carried above them to the great hall. Fires were lit, animals were killed and roasted and pots were filled. Before long, the feast was ready and the drinking and eating began again.

"You've got to tell me, lad," Fiacha said to him over the noise of the singing. "How did you do it? How did you beat the creature?"

Finn thought of all the time he spent learning about music and sound. How would he explain that it was a drum that showed him how to fight the goblin's music? Should he tell Fiacha that he'd wanted to defeat the monster from the Otherworld because he hated Goll so much?

But he knew that the best stories needed a bit of mystery – a bit of magic.

"It was all thanks to my lucky spear," he said to Fiacha.

"I knew it!" Fiacha shouted.

Finn had to tell the story of his fight many times that day and each time he told it, the goblin was more brutal, more cunning and more dangerous. Finn had as much food and drink as one man could eat in a week and then, at the end of the night, he fell into bed. Finn slept for a long, long time and dreamed of becoming a legend.

And today in Ireland, the story is still told of how Finn MacCool defeated the Goblin of Tara and went on to be the greatest Fianna leader that ever lived.

The Legend

This isn't my story. The Goblin of Tara is only one of many myths passed down over the years by Irish storytellers – or seanachaí. Before there were cinemas, TVs or even books, the seanachaí thrilled adults and children long into the night with tales of adventure, comedy and true love.

I made some of the names in this story simpler so that it was easier for those who don't speak any Irish – Fionn MacCumhaill became Finn MacCool, Aillén MacMidhna became MacMeena the Goblin. Anyone who knows Irish will know that 'crac' should be spelled 'craic'. My name Oisín is Irish too – you say it – "Uh-sheen" but you'd never guess that by looking at it.

The Celts came to Ireland in about 300 B.C. They weren't the first to get here but they made a big impression. They spread out over more and more of Northern Europe which made the Romans very angry. The Romans thought the Celts were wild, mad and bad. They got really freaked out when they saw the Celts strip off and charge into battle totally naked! Celtic women would also sometimes fight with their men.

The Romans thought the Celts were too loud, too rude and too fond of arguing. The Celts loved to boast and tell wild stories of battles they had fought. They told tales of magic and giants, demons from the sea.

But the Celts were not savages. They were brave and cunning in battle. They were skilled in metal work, stone-carving and farming. They lived in harmony with nature.

The Celts conquered Ireland but the Romans never did.

They left lots of amazing things for us – their weapons, carvings, and the creepy leathery bog bodies. But it is their stories that make their world come alive for us.

I hope The Goblin of Tara comes alive for you too.

Our books are tested
for children and young people by
children and young people.

Thanks to everyone who consulted on
a manuscript for their time and effort in
helping us to make our books better
for our readers.